# Amalia
## Diary Two

**Other books by
Ann M. Martin**

*P.S. Longer Letter Later*
(written with Paula Danziger)
*Leo the Magnificat*
*Rachel Parker, Kindergarten Show-off*
*Eleven Kids, One Summer*
*Ma and Pa Dracula*
*Yours Turly, Shirley*
*Ten Kids, No Pets*
*Slam Book*
*Just a Summer Romance*
*Missing Since Monday*
*With You and Without You*
*Me and Katie (the Pest)*
*Stage Fright*
*Inside Out*
*Bummer Summer*

THE KIDS IN MS. COLMAN'S CLASS series
BABY-SITTERS LITTLE SISTER series
THE BABY-SITTERS CLUB mysteries
THE BABY-SITTERS CLUB series
CALIFORNIA DIARIES series

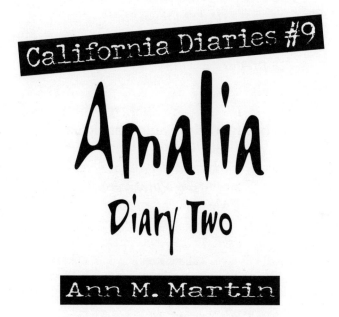

California Diaries #9

# Amalia

## Diary Two

### Ann M. Martin

SCHOLASTIC INC.
New York  Toronto  London  Auckland  Sydney
Mexico City  New Delhi  Hong Kong

*The author gratefully acknowledges
Peter Lerangis
for his help in
preparing this manuscript.*

*Interior illustrations
by
Stieg Retlin*

ISBN 0-590-02385-3

12 11 10 9 8 7 6 5 4 3 2 1                    8 9/9 0 1 2 3/0

Printed in the U.S.A.                    40

First Scholastic printing, October 1998

Nbook, you are not going to believe what magazine I have in front of me.

Teen'zine.

I hate Teen'zine. 99% of the articles are about guys and zits. ("How to Tell Them Apart" might be a truly useful piece.)

I know, I should be doing h.work, not wandering around the periodical rack. But I'm bored.

Anyway, my eye catches a title on the cover, right under "Where Your Favorite Celebs Shop" and "Banish That Blemish":

You Don't Have an Eating Disorder — But Your Friend Does

Well, maybe. I can't help but think about Maggie.

She is so thin, Nbook. Much thinner than when I first met her. And she doesn't eat a thing at lunch.

I'm leafing through the article. It's full of headings and subheadings and testimonials from kids who have survived all these disorders.

Extreme cases. Anorexics who have almost starved themselves to death. Bulimics who wrecked their digestive systems from throwing up too much.

I read about "binge-eating disorder" (out-of-control eating), "anorexia _athletica_" (starving yourself because you're preoccupied with exercise), "night-eating syndrome" (starving during the day but binge-eating at night), "nocturnal sleep-related disorder" (starving during the day but eating in a half-asleep, half-awake state).

Suddenly I feel very full.

The article's pretty hopeful, though. It talks about successful treatment, kids who've gone on to lead normal lives, etc.

Okay. What about Maggie?

Anorexic, or just a nervous stomach?

I don't know.

*Bedtime*
*10:30 or so*

Cut out from <u>Teen'zine</u>, September issue:

---

### *How Can I Tell if My Friend Has an Eating Disorder?*

Answer yes or no.

1. Is your friend preoccupied with food?
2. Is she/he preoccupied with her/his appearance?
3. Does he/she take frequent trips to the restroom?
4. Have you noticed your friend purchasing large amounts of food that vanish quickly?
5. Have you noticed the smell of vomit in the restroom after she/he has used it?

Has your friend:

6. Lost or gained a significant amount of weight?
7. Developed a severe diet or abnormal eating habits?
8. Remained dissatisfied with his/her weight, despite the weight loss?
9. Become socially isolated and/or depressed?

3, 4, and 5 came out _no_.

But in this questionnaire all the eating disorders are lumped together. 3, 4, and 5 refer to bulimia (which Maggie definitely doesn't have) and binge eating (which I've never seen her do).

Every other question, Nbook, is a yes.

So, according to this, Maggie may actually have anorexia.

Hold it.

Don't jump to conclusions, Vargas.

These magazines exaggerate.

I can't believe she's that far gone.


11:53 P.M.
Sleepless in Palo City

Yes, I can.

Thursday, 9/24
7:34 A.M.

Me, zonked but determined

5:01 P.M.

You know what I wish, Nbook? I
wish I knew how to talk. I mean
<u>really</u> talk, not blabber. Express what's
on my mind, with the right words, in
full sentences. The way Sunny and
Dawn do. And of course the way my
beloved sister, Saint Isabel the
Perfect, does.

Maybe I should just <u>draw</u> everything I want to say. Stop talking
completely. Then I'd stay out of trouble.

Today, for instance.

Maggie and I hang out at the Vista
Hills Mall. After reading that article,

I'm looking at her differently than I used to. Noticing things. Like (1) she's constantly gazing at herself in mirrors and sucking in her stomach (such as it is). (2) She changes the subject when I suggest a snack in the food court. (3) She's being really weird about clothes.

We're browsing in Carswell-Hayes. I find this retro '70s skirt — very cool, very Maggie — so I hold it up. She feels the material and makes a face. Then she says, "Too clingy" and turns away.

I'm not expecting this reaction. I mean, clingy dresses are made for figures like Maggie's. And size 4 is plenty big for her, anyway.

This is what I mean, Nbook. She thinks she's too fat. I'm thinking, <u>Is this bizarre or what?</u>

But it's not bizarre at all. It's typical behavior of an anorexic. I know that from the article.

So. Time to talk, right?

Right.

But I don't want to be obvious. I

Figure I'll lead into it gently. In a roundabout way.

I talk about clothes. I talk about movies. TV. CDs. Homework.

We have a lovely conversation. About nothing. Then we go home.

And now I feel like a total chicken.

Me. Loudmouthed, opinionated, honest Amalia.

WHAT IS WRONG WITH ME?

5:21

<u>James</u> is wrong with me. That's what.

He changed me. Made me guarded. Cautious.

True, we didn't go out for very long. True, I broke up with him when he turned into an abusive jerk.

But you know what, Nbook? "Breaking up" is the wrong phrase. You don't break. Not totally. Not when the breakee still wants to get back together. And he sends you notes and puts little unwanted gifts in your locker and stares at you in the hallway and generally makes your life tense and miserable.

After awhile, the fire is sucked out of you.

Well, no more. Today I stop feeling sorry for myself.

Face it, Vargas. Things aren't as bad as they used to be. James is fading. The notes have stopped. He's losing interest. Which is exactly what I've wanted.

No more excuses. It's back to the old Amalia.

I tell Mami my thoughts about Maggie. _She_ says, "It's never too late to talk to her." _I_ say, "I'll take her to dinner at Body-Soul Joy." And _she_ says, "I'll drive you."

I am so glad I have a mom like her.

So I call Maggie right away. B-SJ is supermacrobiotic, low fat, etc., and I'm sure it's about the only restaurant she'll even think of entering.

She says no thanks. But I insist. And I win.

We're meeting there at 6:3φ. Between now and then, I'm going back to that _Teen'zine_ article. Especially the section about how to talk to your friend.

Details tonight.

9:27 P.M.

Everything's perfect. We get a table outside, on the sidewalk, where we can people watch. Leonardo DiCaprio is our waiter (well, a clone, anyway). The smells from the kitchen are making me drool.

I'm a little nervous. The truth is, even though Maggie and I have become pretty good friends, we're just not that close yet. We've never really confided in each other.

I'm trying to ignore all that as Leo brings our menus.

She's embarrassed, uncomfortable. I'm remembering all the stuff I read in <u>Teen'zine</u>. I'm supposed to

- Focus on Maggie, not on her eating.
- Ask questions for clarification.
- Be supportive and caring.
- Understand that recovery is her responsibility, not mine.
- Use "I" statements: "I feel like I'm losing you." "I'm afraid you're going to hurt yourself."

I'm <u>NOT</u> supposed to

- Nag.
- Criticize.
- Pry.
- Control.
- Give advice unless asked.
- Give "You" statements, like "You need help." (Especially stay away from "You're too thin." This is <u>encouraging</u> her, telling her what she wants to hear. Also, for future reference, if she starts <u>gaining</u>, don't say "You look good with some extra weight." She'll just lose the weight again.)

That's all.

Nbook, it's easy enough to write this stuff. But try to remember it while you're having a conversation. <u>Impossible</u>.

Everything's jumbling up in my head. I'm totally tongue-tied.

It doesn't help that practically the whole restaurant can hear us.

So I stand up, take her arm, and we both leave. (Leo gives us a dirty look, but hey, he'll get over it.)

Maggie doesn't say a word until we reach the little park at the end of the block. We sit on a bench, near some sad-looking hedges.

Just like that, Nbook. She admits it.
A BIG step, according to the article.
I'm seeing something I've never
seen before in Maggie. She looks
vulnerable.

The confident, straight-A Girl of a
Million Talents? Gone.

"I — I wasn't sure you knew that,"
I say.

"For a long time I _didn't_," Maggie
replies, "or if I did, I was lying to
myself. Then one night it hit me. My
mom came home incredibly drunk. Like,
staggering. She knocked over the angel
statue in our family room and didn't
even notice the shattered pieces
under her feet. My dad went ballistic.
He told her she needed to face her

drinking problem. But she just stood there and said she didn't _have_ a problem. Just denied it, over and over. So I started thinking, am _I_ like that? Am I doing the same thing?"

"You're not _that_ bad."

(Great work, Vargas. Insult her mom.)

"I don't want to be," Maggie says. "I want to stop before it gets worse. I'm starting to embarrass myself. Like at that restaurant."

"Don't worry. Next time we'll wear masks so the waiter won't recognize us."

Maggie barely cracks a smile. "I was feeling so much _pressure_. All that food going by. Knowing I had to order some."

I'm thinking, _Pressure?_ (Don't worry, Nbook, I don't actually _say_ that.)

"What do you mean?" I ask.

She tells me the vegetarian taco salad is maybe 7¢¢-8¢¢ calories. The whole-wheat rolls in the bread basket are 1¢¢ to 15¢ each, etc. etc. etc. She knows the calorie count for everything.

I suggest she should stop counting, because she looks great and doesn't need to lose any more weight.

She says that _everyone_ tells her that.

"Maybe they have a point," I say as gently as I can.

"Maybe. I mean, I _try_ to believe them. Sometimes I realize I'm being ridiculous. Then I break down and eat something fattening."

"Hey. You're human."

"I don't _feel_ human. I feel disgusting and fat and bloated. I have to skip a few meals just to get back to the way I was."

"You could just pick a weight," I suggest. "You know, a target. Like, 11¢ or something. If you go below it, eat more; if you go above, eat less."

"It's not that easy, Amalia," she snaps. "Targets may work for you, but it's different for me. I have a problem, okay? You don't know what it feels like."

Wrong, Vargas.

Wrong.

Wrong.

I'm contradicting her. Nagging. Giving advice. "You" statements galore. Putting her on the defensive. Getting her mad. Exactly what the article said not to do.

But I notice what she has said. A problem. Those are her words, Nbook.

She really knows how serious it is. And that's important.

Hope. Hope. Hope.

I try to be positive. "Have you talked to anyone about your problem?" I ask.

"You."

"What about your dad and mom?"

Maggie looks at me as if I'm nuts. "My mom hasn't even noticed anything's wrong. Once or twice a week, when

she's sober, she says, 'I am _so_
jealous of your figure.' Dad knows
something's up. He says I'm dieting too
much. But he's the _last_ person I'd
talk to about this."

That is so sad, Nbook. I can't
imagine not going to Mami and Papi with
my problems.

I suggest she talk to her closest
friends. Like Dawn and Ducky. (I
almost mention Sunny, but I don't. Not
the way she's been these days. She
pushes everyone away.)

Maggie nods vaguely. "Maybe."

"One step at a time," I say.

"Yeah," Maggie answers with a tiny,
sad smile.


Late

Don't know what time it is.
Can't sleep.
Thinking about you-know-who.

I was lucky today. I could have
made Maggie worse. I could have lost
a friend forever.

When I jabber away, I say all the wrong things. When I stop to think — when I try to be correct — sometimes I feel so phony. Like I'm trying to recite a textbook page.

Some friend I am.

Maggie's counting on me, Nbook. I'm the only one who knows what's on her mind.

What if she decides not to tell Ducky or Dawn, and I remain her only confidante?

I'm no expert. What if I give her the wrong advice?

I want to talk to Mami and Papi about this. But I can't betray Maggie.

I know what Mami would say: "Be yourself. Don't try to fix her problem — just listen, understand, and empathize."

Papi would say, "Knowledge is power. The more you know, the less you fear."

Okay. I can be a better listener. Empathizer. Whatever.

But I still don't <u>know</u> enough. If I understand her problem, I won't feel like such a dork.

<u>Teen'zine</u> is only a start.
I'll look for other info tomorrow.

Later

Why wait until tomorrow?
The Internet to the rescue.
(Duh. I couldn't have thought of this
before?)
'Bye, Nbook. See you in
cyberspace.

Fri., 9/25
Homeroom

I'm tired.
But I'm wired.
Lots to report. I'm up past 1:00

last night. I download tons of stuff. It's all sitting on my desk.

And I remember it.

Here it is, Nbook, while it's still fresh.

- Anorexia is not only a problem. It's an attempt to solve a <u>perceived</u> problem, even though the "solution" becomes a worse problem.
- Anorexics feel that their lives are out of control. By not eating, they're establishing control — over their bodies.
- Anorexics feel unheard and misunderstood. If you try to change their outlook, even by giving them pep talks, they may feel "talked at." <u>Empathy</u> works best.
- They also feel lots of shame. About their eating. About their

bodies. About all their personal flaws. They need to find out that <u>someone can know the worst about them and still care about them.</u>

- Persistance is important. Recovered anorexics say they appreciate friends and family members who don't give up.

More later.

<u>Anorexia notes</u>

<u>FACT</u>: Eating disorders are tied to personality types. Esp. obsessive-compulsives. (Like MB.)

<u>FACT</u>: Personality types are partly genetic.

<u>THEREFORE</u>: Eating disorders are partly determined genetically.

<u>FACT</u>: Undereating can alter brain chemistry. Creates chemicals that give feeling of peace & happiness, makes habit even worse.

<u>FACT</u>: Anorexics are often perfectionists. Always feel inadequate, no matter how well they do. See things in black & white — "thin is good, thinnest is BEST."

<u>FACT</u>: They may have lots of anger but don't express it, because they want approval. So they turn the anger <u>inward</u>. Undereating is a form of anger at self.

<u>FACT</u>: They often come from success-oriented, pressured families — with parents who the kid feels are <u>very critical</u>.

FA

That was not fun. You were almost confiscated in class, Nbook.

But I saved you.

Anyway, here's the <u>FACT</u> I was going to mention next before I was so rudely interrupted:

Sometimes a "trigger event" can get an anorexic started.

Like a new, unreasonable demand.

Well, guess what? Maggie Blume has a whole life of trigger events.

And it's not only family and school. She totally blew her big chance with her #1 crush, Justin Randall. I'm not entirely sure what happened. I can guess, though. I'm sure it had to do with Maggie's state of mind. Justin's a good guy, but how long can he be interested in a girl who's so hard on herself?

I'd be a basket case if this were me.

I don't know, Nbook. Maybe the girl's in more trouble than I thought.

study hall

Dear ~~Jerk~~ ~~Idiot~~ ~~Hateful Person~~ James,

I don't know how you managed to open my locker.

I assume you were the one who put rose petals in my sketchbook.

First of all, I hate red roses.

They're boring. Plus, they stain. And you got them all over the place. In my science textbook. In my sneakers. Everywhere.

If you ~~do~~ that again, I will call the ~~police~~ assistant principal.

You are a ~~menace~~ ~~threat~~ ~~pain in the~~

I end up not sending the letter.

I show it to Ducky after school. He's as angry as I am. He can't believe James is at it again.

But he tells me to work on the text more. He thinks it needs to be nastier.

Ducky hates James. Which makes perfect sense. James disses him all the time.

I will never understand why James does that. I mean, how can <u>anyone</u> diss Ducky? Because he doesn't act macho and dress like everyone else? Because he has an outrageous laugh and a wild sense of humor? He is totally adorable — always asking how you are, always trying to help out. So different from James "Enough about me, now let's discuss how _you_ feel about me" Kodaly.

After school today, for instance, when Ducky sees me walking home, he _insists_ on giving me a ride.

As we drive off, he puts on WPCZ, full blast. We're both singing along. Gossiping. Laughing.

I'm feeling so relaxed. Ducky's putting me at ease. Saying all the right things.

And then it occurs to me — _Maggie_ should be here. She should be confiding in Ducky, not me.

He knows how to talk. He can ask questions without being obnoxious. Give advice without seeming to. Listen and listen and listen, as if you are the most important person in the world.

Maybe I'm just the wrong person for Maggie.

I almost tell about Maggie's problem. But I stop myself.

I can't. That would be betraying her. Talking behind her back.

She has to be the one to approach him.

Ducky stops in front of the house. I invite him inside. I figure, it's Friday, his parents are still in Ghana, he's probably facing another night of macaroni & ketchup with his brother. And I'm sure Mami and Papi won't mind having him over for dinner. Simon Big Tooth Lover Boy freeloads all the time. (OK, he's Isabel's boyfriend, but still.)

But Ducky's face darkens when I ask him to stay. He says he can't. He has to go to his friend Alex's. For "damage control." Meaning Alex is depressed and needs all the friends he can get.

I tell him Alex is lucky to have him as a friend.

Ducky appreciates that. It shows in his face.

Hmm.

What do you think, Nbook?
Me and Ducky?
Nahh.

4:31 P.M.

Maybe.

4:57

Nahh.

6:09

Nbook, I'm scared. And annoyed.
    The first time the phone rings, I
figure it's Rico canceling tomorrow's
rehearsal or something.
    When the person on the other end
hangs up, I don't think much about it.
    The second time it happens, I'm a
little creeped.
    I mean, it should be no big deal,
right? Just a hang-up.
    But I'm all alone. Mami and Papi
are at their offices. Isabel's working
at the women's shelter.

And suddenly I'm running around the house, making sure the doors are locked.

The third time, I'm angry.

I pick up and yell, "Who is this?"

Then, <u>click</u>.

I slam the phone down and wish we had Caller ID.

Then I remember what Isabel does every time she misses a phone call and thinks it was Simon. She presses a code and the phone automatically calls back the person who last reached her.

I try it.

"Hello?"

It's Marina. (Remember her, Nbook, sister of James and former good friend?)

I freeze. I am totally tongue-tied. But not entirely surprised.

I <u>know</u> I should say, "Your brother the jerk is harassing me over the phone again."

But I don't want to drag Marina into it. He's practically ruined our friendship. This would just upset her and make things worse.

So I pretend I just called her casually. I ask if she's coming to the vanish rehearsal.

"Am I supposed to?" she asks.

"Nope. Just wondering."

End of conversation. Good-bye, hang up. Nbook, I hate being dishonest.

I stand there forever. I can't decide whether or not to call her back.

And then the phone rings again.

This time I wait for the answering machine. It picks up after the fourth ring.

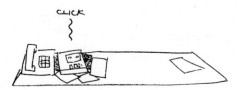

I ignore it.

I run upstairs.

I jump into bed and bury my head under a pillow.

The phone rings again. And again.

Each time, the machine takes it.

Each time, there's no message.

This is embarrassing.

I'm running around, fixing things, setting up a tape recorder so we can hear what rehearsal sounds like, basically being a good manager. James is the farthest thing from my mind.

And I notice everyone's laughing at me.

Rico starts playing some dumb song on his guitar. Justin joins in, singing "Tiptoe Through the Tulips." Bruce picks up the bass, Patti hits the drumset, and Maggie plays along on the keyboard.

I think they've all gone nuts. Then I look at the floor.

Rose petals are scattered at my feet. They have fallen out of my folder. I must have missed them in my big rose petal cleanup.

I hold in my temper. I calmly pick

up the petals. I explain where they came from.

The moment I mention James, everyone reacts angrily.

Patti goes off about "girlfriend abuse."

Bruce says, "Kicking him out of the group was the best thing we ever did."

"We should have tarred and feathered him," Rico declares.

And the weird thing is, I'm feeling <u>relieved</u>. Somewhere in my mind I've been thinking they all hate <u>me</u>, not him.

Let's face it, it's my fault that Vanish lost a good guitar player.

## THE DOWNFALL OF VANISH

Justin is OK. But he's still learning. And, as much as I hate to admit it, I don't think he has James's talent.

"We sound better without James," Patti is saying.

Everyone agrees.

And I don't argue.

VANISH, 9/26, 5:00

Nbook, I can't watch this.

I try to talk to Maggie after rehearsal. But Bruce and Rico pull me aside.

What is this, Nbook?

Like I really need this? I'm so fragile I need protection?

Please.

You know what? It's not just James I'm sick of.

It's guys in general.

# FURTHER NOTES ON GUYS & UNTRUST-
## WORTHINESS

Just random, unscientific observations.
Not to be made public.

- They say "talk" when they mean "threaten."
- They hate to cry. (How can you trust someone who won't cry?)
- Everything is a contest. Even relationships.
- If they think they're losing, they either bail out or make you think that you did something wrong.
- "Giving" means "expecting something in return."
- "Sympathizing" means "looking for an excuse to play hero."

Okay, not <u>all</u> guys are like this.
Ducky's not.
But he doesn't count. He's an exception.

From this moment on, Nbook, I am declaring a new policy.

No More Guys.

I hereby swear them off.

Forever.

Monday, 9/28
8:01 A.M.

Great news.

Dawn calls me at 7:45. She's all breathless.

Maggie finally talked to her last night. Phoned her out of the blue.

She told Dawn everything. The eating problem. Her mom and the statue. The pressures.

Plus, Maggie admitted that she's talked to me too. She swore Dawn to secrecy, but she doesn't mind if Dawn and I discuss her problem. "Let's just keep it in the family," she tells Dawn.

Family.

I guess that's what we are.

Families care. Stick together. Support and love each other.

   She's reaching out, Nbook.

   I'm not the only one anymore.

   WHAT

   A

   RELIEF!

   Dawn's pretty upset, though. She'd already suspected Maggie had a problem, but you know Dawn. Always looking on the bright side. She figured it was just a diet that went on too long.

   I spend a lot of time telling her what I've learned about anorexia.

   We talk about ways to help Maggie, but we don't get too far because we both have to leave.

   But I finally feel like I'm doing something useful.


## Homeroom

   Dawn's call makes me late. I rush into homeroom. Mr. Leavitt's back is turned, so I try to slide into my seat.

Only <u>this</u> is sitting here.

"You're in my seat!" I whisper harshly.

The guy looks startled.

I've never seen him before.

He's kind of cute. His eyes are so <u>green</u>.

Mr. Leavitt turns around and says, "Ah, Amalia. Our last guest. The party can begin."

I hate sarcastic teachers.

"Sorry," the guy with the eyes says. He's fumbling with his stuff, gathering it up. "I'll move."

Now I feel awful. I tell him to stay put. It's OK. I sit in back, near Cece.

I'm sure the guy hates me now. Some introduction to Palo City hospitality.

Mr. Leavitt has just welcomed New Boy.

He's Brendan Jones. Formerly of Short Hills, New Jersey.

Cool name. (Brendan, not Short Hills.)

He seems pretty quiet.

Cece passes me a note. Three words: BRENDAN = CUTE + MYSTERIOUS.

I give her a look.

She scribbles another one: WEIRD TIME TO SWITCH SCHOOLS, ISN'T IT? PEOPLE MOVE AT THE BEGINNING OF THE SCHOOL YEAR.

To tell the truth, I hadn't even thought of that. And who cares?

Typical Cece comment. A mountain out of a molehill.

Personally, I think she's hot for this guy.

c —

Maybe his family had trouble getting here.

I never send Cece the note. The homeroom bell rings too soon.

I'm feeling guilty about yelling at Brendan, so I decide to apologize to him.

But I'm too late.

Rowena Frank has gotten there first. And she's yapping away: "As your student government president and cool-girl wanna-be, I'm supposed to show you around and impress you . . ."

Well, something like that.

She walks confidently out of the classroom. Brendan trails behind.

Cece and I are trying not to laugh as we leave the room.

Then I see James.

He's standing in the shadow of the lockers. Staring at me. Not even smiling.

Cece and I stop laughing. We walk past him.

So now I'm thinking <u>Is he mad? Did something happen? Did Rico or Bruce</u>

"talk to him"? Did they say something stupid?

Do I need to be careful?

Math

Just back from lunch.

Got 2 write fast. Ms. Sevekow on warpath.

Dawn & I meet Maggie on lunch line.

We're picking out food. D & I keeping our mouths shut. No pressure for M.

M is having rough time. Takes salad
from rack but brushes off egg slice &
avocado. Reaches for roll, puts it
back. Eyes the granola bars but
doesn't even try.

M notices we're looking at her.
Smiles & turns red.

D says the veggie sandwich is good.
M stares at it for second & says, "I'll
try it."

We all leave the line. Sit.

D & I eat. M looks tense. Takes
a bite of sandwich and makes a
face. As if she just bit into a mouse
tail.

"There's mayonnaise," she says.

We say oh.

She shrugs.

We shrug.

No one knows what to say next.

Finally M breaks into a big,
embarrassed smile. "Sorry, guys. This is
hard." This meaning eating.

Cool. We understand.

Sorry, had to stop.

Now it's lab report time. I can write for real.

Where was I?

Lunch. Maggie admits she's having a hard time.

I say, "I see you're trying." (See? An "I" sentence.)

She seems upset. "I don't like the way this feels."

"What?" Dawn asks.

"The eating, the pressure, all of it," Maggie replies. "I can't do this, guys."

Now, I <u>know</u> I'm not supposed to give advice, Nbook. But I want to. The look on Maggie's face is breaking my heart. So I think about what Mami would do in this situation. She meets lots of troubled kids in her social work. When things get really serious, she refers them to a psychologist. This friend of hers. I forget her name, but she's supposed to be fantastic.

I can't keep it in. "Maybe you should see someone," I say. "Like a therapist."

Maggie sighs. "Both my parents see therapists and it doesn't do them any good."

"How about a teacher?" Dawn asks. "Or a guidance counselor?"

"No," says Maggie. "I can't talk to anyone in the school. Then <u>everyone</u> will find out."

"How about your doctor?" I suggest. (I mean, anorexia IS a medical problem.)

"Dr. Fradkin still gives me lollipops at the end of checkups," Maggie replies. "Besides, he and Dad play golf."

Dawn and I fall silent.

The bell rings.

End of discussion.


P.S. She doesn't eat the rest of the sandwich.

But she has a few bites of the salad.

Oh, well.

One.

Step.

At.

A.

Time.

I can't even concentrate the rest of the day.

After science I see Dawn with Maggie in the hallway. Brendan lopes past us. He's being led around by Rowena like a Chihuahua.

He's kind of cute. Not drop-dead-hunk cute, but sort of slouchy-nice-guy cute. I wish he'd smile more. He never looks happy.

Maybe that's because he's always around Rowena.

Maggie says, "You know him?"

"Not really," I answer. "Why?"

"He smiled at you." She raises an eyebrow. "He likes you, Amalia."

A joke. Maggie's sense of humor is coming back. This is a good sign.

I tell her my current Theory of Guys. I make it totally clear that I am so <u>over</u> them. Brendan is no exception, jesting or not. He is nobody.

But now Maggie and Dawn are both laughing at me.

I shut my mouth and take it.

I don't mind.

Much.

Back again
Still study hall

Oh, by the way. The eyes are bluish, not all green.

Not that it matters.

I'm just reporting.

Big news, Nbook.

Big BIG news.

It's after school. I'm just about to slam my locker shut and run out, when I feel a hand on my shoulder.

Oh, great, I think.

James.

I'm angry. I don't know what I'm capable of doing.

I spin around.

It's not James. It's Christina McDonnell.

What a relief.

What a surprise.

A nice one. I don't know her, but I've always wanted to. She seems cool. Friendly. Pretty. Popular.

She asks if I'm the manager of Vanish. When I say yes, she brightens right up. She says she's a big fan. She saw us at the Battle of the Bands and we deserved first place.

Then she says something like, "I know this is short notice, and I'm sure your schedule is too busy — but is there a chance you could play the Vista Homecoming Bash on the 10th?"

I'm thinking, a _job_? Us?

The _yes_ rushes out of my throat so fast I choke on it.

Christina explains that the Bash isn't really a _date_ party. People will be coming in groups, mostly. A DJ will play tunes after our set.

Cool, I say.

She goes on to say that she already approached Rico about this, and he said that I handle the pay arrangements and scheduling.

_Pay?_

I blurt out, "We're free!"

_Idiot!_ I'm screaming to myself.

But Christina has misunderstood me. She thinks, _free_ as in _available_. She's writing in her datebook. "Good. I'll pencil you in. Now, what's your normal fee?"

I'm not even rational. I'm not thinking. Part of me wants to laugh. Part of me wants to offer to pay _her_.

A third part of me pushes the other parts aside.

It says $50¢.

I have no idea where that came from. I'm in shock.

I think Christina's going to faint. I think I'm going to faint.

I'm about to say "Just kidding," but she speaks first.

"It's a deal."

A deal?

I'm stunned.

I'm about to scream hallelujah.

But I'm also the manager, and I have to look after my group's best interests. So I tell her I'll have to check it out with the band at rehearsal tonight and then get back to her tomorrow.

Can you believe this, Nbook?

Our first paying gig!

I'M FLOATINNNNGGGG!

Long night.

Where to begin?

Okay. Start at the good part.

Mami drives me to Rico's. But because she came home late from work, I'm the last one at the rehearsal.

I notice Justin hanging out with Bruce at the snack table ("the trough," as Mr. Chavez calls it). I see Maggie playing keyboard, ignoring him. This is not good. I make a mental note to talk to her later.

Then I see Rico. He's grinning.

I assume he's told everyone about Christina's offer. But no one seems excited.

Suddenly he jacks up his amp and strikes a loud TWWANNNNNG! on his guitar.

"Yo, listen up, everybody! Amalia has a big announcement!"

He's left all the glory to me. (I love Rico. Even if he is a guy.)

I jump onto the platform and grab Maggie's mike. She's giving me this curious look.

Everyone bursts into wild applause when I tell them about the gig.

I save the part about the money for last.

When they hear that, they're screaming. Jumping on me. Hugging me. Lifting me off the ground.

"I said 5¢, not 5¢,¢¢¢!" I shout.

No one cares. I could have said 5¢, and they'd be happy.

Rico starts playing "For She's a Jolly Good Fellow." His parents announce they're getting ice cream and snacks to celebrate. I'm feeling fantastic.

Then I look at Maggie.

She's still at the keyboard. Sitting. Her brow is all wrinkled.

When she sees me, she smiles. But I'm not fooled.

Something's wrong.

I wait until snack break to approach her. By that time, we've

settled into rehearsal and played
through a few songs.

While everyone is pigging out,
Maggie's off in a corner with a bottle
of spring water.

I ask her if she's OK.

Fine, fine.

I want to say something about her
eating, but this isn't the right time. So
I remark that she seems to be
ignoring Justin.

She shrugs. She says they're still
friends, just her crush on him is over.
No big deal.

We sit. She sips.

Finally I ask how she feels about
the Homecoming Bash.

Her face tightens up. "Great
news," she says quietly.

"Don't knock me over with your
excitement," I say.

I mean it as a joke. But Maggie
doesn't smile. She tells me the date
is too soon. She doesn't feel ready.

I remind her she knows the
numbers cold.

She tells me it's not just a question of _knowing_. The songs need _rewriting_. The bridge to "Slow Down," the second verse of this, the third verse of that . . .

I assure her they're fine and no one will notice.

"I notice," she replies. "They're _my_ words. I can't sing them if they stink. I have enough trouble singing anything these days. I'm straining above middle C. Maybe I'm getting a node on my throat. I'll be lucky if I have a voice by the Homecoming Bash."

"Maggie, you just need to relax," I say.

"Easy for you to say. You don't have to make a fool of yourself before the whole school. You're not tired all the time because you can't eat right. You don't have to worry about looking fat —"

"You're not fat!"

Once again, wrong, wrong, _wrong,_ _WRONG_ thing to say.

"It's too much pressure, Amalia. Okay?"

Justin and Bruce are looking at us now.

Maggie storms away.

I pretend to be busy with my set list.


Well, Maggie comes back and plays the rest of the rehearsal. She's such a good actress. She doesn't let her bad mood show at all.

On her way out after rehearsal she apologizes to me. Then she disappears into the waiting limo.

I try to be UP, but I feel awful.

At home, I call Dawn and tell her what happened. She thinks Maggie will get over it. She reminds me that anorexia is about low self-esteem, and maybe the Bash will be just the thing to turn it around for Maggie.

Maybe.

Unless it goes the other way.

All night long I'm worrying that she's backsliding.

That's another thing I learned on

the Internet. Sometimes an anorexic's recovery can be like a roller coaster — the condition can get worse just when it seems to be getting better.

After I talked to Dawn tonight, I almost called Maggie. But it was already too late.

Or so I thought.

I was stupid.

I should have called her.

It's definitely out of the question now.

Way to go, Vargas.

Night
Or morning
Hard to tell

NOTE FOR Tomorrow:
¡¡DR. FUENTES!!
That's the name of the therapist.
Ask Mami about her.

Plan of ~~attack~~ action:

Push the idea of Dr. Fuentes. But don't push too hard.

Just tell the truth. Say what Mami said. Dr. F is one of the coolest women on the planet. She's young. She's a great listener. She's a pro. She doesn't talk down to kids. She's practically one of us.

You can't get a better recommendation than that.

Study hall

Lots to tell.

The minor news first.

I see James before school. He doesn't look at me.

I see him after homeroom. He walks the other way.

Maybe he's given up.

Hooray.

OK, enough ink wasted on that.

The important news:

Morning. Before school. Lockers.

First, Christina rushes up to me and asks about Vanish's decision.

When I tell her yes, she's <u>thrilled</u>. And guess what? She already has a presigned check for $5¢¢ and she gives it to me ON THE SPOT.

I'm staring at the check as Christina leaves. Like it's radioactive. I have <u>never</u> held so much $$!

Both Dawn and Maggie are making faces. Like, <u>what a big shot</u>.

I calmly tell them I'm going to take the money and go to Mexico tonight.

I'm joking, but you know, Nbook, it wouldn't be a bad idea. . . .

Anyway, that's not the <u>real</u> important news.

That happens next.

I'm noticing Maggie's in a better mood. She apologizes again for what she said at rehearsal last night. She says she was so mad at herself, she went home and cried herself to sleep.

I forgive her.

Dawn's very sympathetic: "The Homecoming Bash is a big deal ... no wonder you were tense ... it's a lot of pressure ...," etc.

Maggie says she's thinking of taking a yoga class. To ease the stress.

I decide to open the Big Subject. "Can I make a suggestion?"

"Anything," Maggie says.

I say I've thought of a great person for her to talk to. I tell her about Dr. Fuentes.

Dawn's nodding, trying to look positive. But Maggie's not saying a thing.

So I figure she's feeling pushed. Drop back and punt, or whatever that saying is. Time to change the subject.

Only I can't think of another subject to change to, and I can see the panic starting to creep into Dawn's face —

And suddenly the bell rings.

"I'll think about it," Maggie says.

We run off to class.


Uh-uh. It's not over.

Next time I see her, it's lunch.

Dawn and I sit at her table. She's picking at a salad.

She starts firing questions — where

does Dr. Fuentes live, how old is she, what are her credentials, etc.

My heart is sinking. I know Maggie. She's looking for a flaw. One strike and Dr. Fuentes is out.

I answer everything and then Maggie falls silent again.

"It's worth a try," Dawn says meekly. "Isn't it?"

"This therapist doesn't know me," Maggie finally replies. "Or my teachers or my family."

"But that's _good_," Dawn insists.

I give her a look that means, _Go easy on her_.

But Maggie says, "I _know_ it's good. That's what I meant. She's a stranger. You pay her to listen and she keeps your secrets."

I don't expect to hear this.

Neither does Dawn.

"I could call her," I say tentatively. "You know, set up an appointment . . ."

Maggie sighs. "I guess . . ."

Don't worry, Nbook. I don't jump up and dance on the table.

But I want to.

Even _more_ news. Late-breaking headline:

Well, a little. He's VERY shy.

But today I had this conversation with him. After study hall.

He's in the hallway, looking kind of lost. I feel sorry for him. I say hi. No big deal.

He actually _blushes_.

Anyway, we're going the same direction, so we start walking together. I'm doing most of the talking (surprise, surprise). We get to the topic of the

Homecoming Bash, and of course I put in a plug for you-know-who.

"My group is playing," I say.

Brendan lights up. Big smile. Nice one too. "Are you a singer?"

"Only in the shower."

Oops. Brendan is embarrassed again. I didn't know blood could rush to a face so fast. It's kind of adorable in a way. I almost break out laughing.

"I'm the manager," I say with a straight face.

"Cool," he says. "Hard job, huh? Do all the work, get none of the credit."

Smart too.

I like that.

Not that it matters.

He is, after all, a guy.

Tonight, if I have time, I'll make him a copy of the tape I made at rehearsal.

I call Dr. Fuentes as soon as I get home. She can see Maggie after school tomorrow. I set up the appointment.

Right away I call Maggie. She's very quiet. One-word answers.

OK, I'm not expecting her to gush, but still, I can't tell how she's feeling. Is she mad at me? Is she changing her mind?

"It's the right thing," I say.

"Okay."

"You'll be glad you did it."

"I guess."

"You still <u>want</u> to, right?"

"Sure, sure. Look, I can't really talk now. There are people around. Plus, I have to finish the social studies report and clean the mess in my room. And my dad needs me to fax him some papers. So we'll talk later, OK?"

"OK. See you."

"'Bye."

She's incredible, Nbook. So hard-working. And so _good_ at everything — piano, singing, poetry, schoolwork, songwriting. She's a good person. A good friend. A good daughter and sister.

But you know what the problem is? She's not _perfect_. And that bothers her.

I've been trying to tell her she's great just the way she is. So has Dawn.

But she's so lost in her own feelings. I don't think she really hears.

Which is exactly why she needs a pro. Someone who's trained to listen and say the right thing.

I hope Dr. Fuentes is all she's cracked up to be.

_Way_ cool.
I am totally blown away.

The Homecoming Bash posters are up. Already.

When did Christina do this? After school yesterday, I guess.

The girl does NOT let grass grow under her feet.

Nbook, they're gorgeous. And Vanish's name is splashed across the bottom, in HUGE letters like this:

PLAYING LIVE at the Homecoming Bash

This morning, in the lobby, everyone's gathering around it. Rico is going nuts. Bruce and Patti are trying to be cool about it, but I can tell they're thrilled. Even Maggie has a smile on her face.

I am so PROUD.

I mean, just yesterday we're this garage band, Nbook. Playing music for fun. Hanging out. Nobody to hear us but ourselves.

Then comes the Battle of the Bands. And now this. We're <u>pros</u>!
What next? THE SKY'S THE LIMIT!

I visit the poster again after homeroom.

Maggie's there too. We gush. Kids are passing by, saying they're happy that Vanish is playing. All very good for the ego.

Then Maggie's smile does a slow fade.

From behind me, I hear Justin's voice saying, "Hey, cool" or something.

He's nodding.

I nod.

Maggie nods.

We look like strange tropical birds in the zoo.

After some small talk, we all go off to class.

I have a hunch, Nbook.

He still likes her. She still likes him.

But something's _off_. They need to work it out.

Maybe Dr. Fuentes does couples therapy.

Math

Today at lunch Maggie's even more nervous than usual.

She's having second thoughts. About Dr. Fuentes.

"Are you sure this is a good idea?" she asks.

Dawn and I exchange a look.

I repeat what Mami has said about Dr. Fuentes.

"But what if it's _not_ that big a problem?" Maggie asks. "What if I can solve it myself? If I go to the therapist, I might be making the whole thing bigger than it is. And then it could take <u>longer</u> to get over it."

"Well, uh . . ." What can I say, Nbook? I <u>know</u> she needs this. But I don't want to force her to do something she's not ready for.

"I'm sure you'll make the right decision," Dawn says.

Thank you, Dawn.

She's absolutely right.

Maggie needs to decide, not me.

She better decide right.

If she cancels, I don't know what I'll do.

Science

After math, just outside of class, Cece pulls me aside and asks what's the matter. She says I'm looking depressed.

We start walking. I begin to tell her what's happening — without mentioning Maggie's name.

Then she elbows me in the ribs.

Just because Brendan is heading toward us.

He says hi. I say hi.

He falls into step with us.

I reach into my pocket. I pull out the copy of the Vanish rehearsal tape I made last night, and I give it to him.

He lights up. "Cool. I'll give it back tomorrow."

"It's yours," I say.

"Thanks."

He's genuinely excited.

Cece's raising her eyebrows. "A gift," she says meaningfully.

Brendan and I politely ignore her. We talk music.

And then I see HIM.

James the Unruly.

He's standing against the wall. Giving me the eye.

Guess he's decided to remember who I am after all. Funny how he only does that whenever I'm with another guy.

He's jealous. It's obvious.

If it weren't James, I might be flattered.

I mean, jealousy means someone cares about you, right?

Not with James. He thinks that once I've been his girlfriend, I couldn't <u>possibly</u> be attracted to anyone else.

Like I care about Brendan, anyway.

Like I care at all.

Maggie the yo-yo.

Just now, in the hallway, she tells me she's been thinking about the session all day.

"Are you going?" I ask.

She gives me a funny look. "I never said I wasn't."

Yes.

"So . . . I'll meet you after school?" I ask.

"Yeah. See you."

She looks so sad as she walks off,

Nbook. As if I'm taking her to a
funeral.

Have I forced her into this?

Now even I'm starting to have doubts.

This Is the right choice
This Is the right choice
This Is the right choice
This Is the right choice
This Is the right choice
This Is the right choice

9:14 P.M.

I'm exhausted.

But I have to write this down,
Nbook. Even if it takes me all night.

OK. I'm in the hallway after school.
Waiting for Maggie. I see Ducky. He
offers me a ride home.

I don't want to tell him where I'm
going, which would lead to why. So I
say no.

Then Maggie shows up. She's looking
all glum and tortured. I can tell she's
afraid. Still second-guessing.

"Girl, what's with _you_?" Ducky asks.

"Nothing," Maggie mumbles.

Please please please don't pry, I'm thinking.

Next thing you know, we're all in his car. Me in the back, them in the front.

"Maggie first," I say. I call out Dr. Fuentes's address.

Ducky, of course, is Ducky. He knows that's not where Maggie lives, and he can't stop asking questions. Who are you visiting? Anyone I know?

Maggie's giving him short answers. Changing the subject.

Ducky's saying, A doctor? A dentist? A spiritual healer? A boyfriend?

I'm cringing.

Finally Maggie says, "A therapist, all right? I'm going to see a therapist. But that's between us three and Dawn."

"Oh." Ducky nods. "Cool beans."

Nobody says anything for awhile. Good old Ducky has sized up the situation. He knows he needs to back off.

Finally he says, "It would be great to know about a new therapist."

Maggie looks concerned. "Are you having problems too?"

"No," Ducky says. "I'm fine. It's for Alex. For future reference. He's been playing musical therapists. One of these days he'll find someone who works. So I'm collecting names."

I'm thinking, Hey, I should be a referral service.

We pull up to Dr. Fuentes's house. It's medium-size. Nice. The office is in a small wing off to the side.

Maggie steps out. Ducky and I wish her good luck.

"We'll pick you up," Ducky volunteers. "How long's the session?"

"Forty-five minutes," I say.

Maggie's staring at me. She looks scared. "You're not leaving."

A statement. Not a question.

"I'm not?"

"No way, Amalia. I need you."

I know I should drive off with

Ducky. For Maggie's own good. This is
her life, her session. She'll be stronger
if she faces her problems on her own.
She may want to admit things to Dr.
Fuentes that she wouldn't admit to me.

But panic is shooting across her
face. Panic and fear and surprise. As
if I'm betraying her. Abandoning her.

I can't bear to leave her like that.

So I stay.

We wave to Ducky as he drives
off.

We walk up the path, through the
office door, and into a small waiting
room.

No one else is there. Just a stack
of magazines on a coffee table. Off to
the side, behind a closed door, we
hear muffled voices. A white-noise
machine is hissing on the floor, but it
doesn't block out all the sound.

Maggie paces.

I sit and pretend to read
magazines.

Soon Dr. Fuentes's patient leaves. A
few moments later, Dr. Fuentes leans

out of her office door. She's dressed
in a rust-and-gold silk patterned skirt
and a billowy white blouse. Her eyes
are big and still and brown, her smile
warm and wide.

She asks Maggie in, making sure to
say hi to me. Then she begins to
close the door.

"Uh, can she come in too?" Maggie
asks.

"Perhaps you'd feel freer if you
were alone," Dr. Fuentes says.

"No," Maggie answers. "I won't. I
know it."

Dr. Fuentes looks at me.

I'm standing there, <u>duh</u>.

"Well, it's not my usual procedure,"
Dr. Fuentes says. "But if Amalia has
the time . . ."

"OK," I squeak.

Maggie smiles. I walk in. There
are two seats and a kind of bed/sofa
thing, no back cushions, just a big
headrest and pillow at one end.

Dr. Fuentes sits on one of the
seats, Maggie on the other.

The only one who's relaxed is Dr. Fuentes.

Now what? I'm supposed to lie on the bed?

I sit on it. At the edge.

I feel like <u>I'm</u> the one in therapy.

A minute or two of small talk, then Dr. Fuentes opens a notebook and takes a pen in hand.

Maggie starts talking.

And talking.

I'm waiting for the Tale of Gloom &

Blume, and she's yakking away as if life is great.

She's telling Dr. Fuentes about the good stuff. The adventures of her brother, Zeke. Her pets. Her school projects. Her songwriting. <u>Inner Vistas</u>, the school literary magazine she edits.

Dr. Fuentes seems totally entertained.

Me too. I feel like I'm beginning to know her more.

Maggie moves on to the details of her life. Her piano lessons, her singing, Vanish, the Battle of the Bands.

And I'm beginning to realize something.

She's stalling.

She's here to talk about a problem, and she hasn't even touched the subject.

I look at the clock. 37 minutes have gone by. The session is supposed to last only 45.

Dr. Fuentes hasn't said much at all. Just "Mm-hm" and "Well!" and "How does that make you feel?"

Finally, when Maggie runs out of

breath, Dr. Fuentes puts down her notebook. "Maggie, it sounds to me like a wonderful life."

Maggie nods.

"I mean, what 13-year-old girl wouldn't trade with you in a minute?"

Maggie nods again.

"The glamour. The parties. The music. I'd say you were a lucky kid."

No.

This can't be happening.

My stomach is sinking.

This is her therapy?

Telling Maggie that her life is perfect? Things aren't as bad as they seem?

They _are_ bad. That's the point.

LOOK AT HER BODY! I want to scream out.

It's dawning on me that Dr. Fuentes is just like everyone else. She sees a rich girl and assumes that nothing could possibly be the matter.

And I'm thinking Mami was wrong. Going to Dr. Fuentes is a big, big mistake.

I'm not done yet.

But I'm beat. More tomorrow, Nbook.

Back again.

Where was I?

Dr. Fuentes's office.

Maggie has just been told things are great.

She doesn't like this at all. Her smile vanishes.

What _is_ everything, Maddie?

A functional family. A house with some privacy, where Hollywood people in power suits and power tans aren't wandering around, drooling over the antiques. A dad who comes home before midnight once in a while. A mom who doesn't wake you up at 3 A.M. so drunk she can't see.

A life without always _performing_: "Play the Chopin, Maddie... sing for Mr Franz ... go get your haiku that won the contest, bring us your report card..." A day that you can be lazy and not think about the _other_ kids who are pulling ahead of you because they're working hard at that moment. A day when you don't worry about your singing voice, your hair, your skin, your fat—

fat.

She says it just like that. Gently. Not a question, not a ridicule. Just a word.

"That's how I feel," Maggie explains. "I . . . have this problem with eating. It's like torture to me. I hate the sight of food. I hate the sight of myself. When I was 110, I wanted to be 105. When I was 105, I wanted to be 100. I feel like nothing comes easy to me — not weight, not school, not friends. . . ."

"Maggie," Dr. Fuentes says, "what <u>does</u> come easily to you? What do you really <u>enjoy</u>?"

Maggie thinks a moment. "Writing. My poems. My songs. I mean, I'm not that <u>good</u> at it, but I love it. I get lost in myself. Like I'm in a private little room where everything's perfect." She sighs. "Sometimes I just wish I could stay there."

"Why don't you?"

"I can't be lazy all the time. I have work to do. You can't be the best if you're locked away from reality."

"And you have to be the best."

"I try."

"And what happens if you're not the best?"

Maggie's looking annoyed. "I don't think about that."

"The world would end?"

"No. But things would . . . I don't know, fall apart."

"Your grades?"

"Yes."

"Your lessons?"

"Yes."

"Your band?"

"Yes."

"Your family?"

"Yes."

"Your body too?"

Maggie opens her mouth to say yes. But nothing comes out.

I can tell the comment has hit home. Her eyes have become red.

"You don't get it," Maggie says. "You don't have my family. You don't have the pressure of —"

"Of what? Of having to fix things? Of

having to make it all better? Being the shining star? The one who makes everyone smile? 'We Blumes may be falling apart, but <u>Maggie's</u> acing her exams and playing a recital and singing in a band and winning awards and looking thin and beautiful.' Is that it?"

Maggie's shoulders heave a bit. She shudders.

<u>Don't cry</u>, I'm thinking.

Maggie is a rock. She never lets her anger or sadness or frustration show. Seeing her like this is scary.

Then I realize something, Nbook. Now <u>I'm</u> being like everyone else. I'm expecting her to be perfect.

"You don't like to cry, do you?" Dr. Fuentes asks softly.

Maggie shakes her head.

"You hate when everything feels out of control. Especially your emotions."

Maggie nods.

Then, finally, she breaks down into sobs. Kind of pent up and squeaky at first, then louder until she's practically gasping for air.

I walk over to her and put my arm around her shoulder. We rock back and forth. I'm pretty weepy myself.

I know it's time to end the session, but Dr. Fuentes doesn't mention it.

Finally Maggie says, in a tiny voice, "You're right."

"Maggie, some things are beyond our control," Dr. Fuentes says softly. "You can't solve everyone's problems. Yours are hard enough."

"I want to get better," Maggie says.

Dr. Fuentes nods. "I believe you. You're here. That means you want to change. Which is a good thing. Because anorexia can be very serious."

Maggie blanches. "What can I do?"

"First of all, realize it may take awhile," Dr. Fuentes replies. "What's causing the problem — the tension, the family trouble — none of that will magically disappear."

"Which means what? I won't get better until it does?"

"No. You can get better. In our next session, we'll begin mapping out a plan. To put Maggie first. Friday sound okay?"

"Sure," Maggie shoots back.

"Meanwhile, try not to be so hard on yourself, Maggie. That's step one. And remember, we're born to eat. Our bodies want food, and they deserve it."

"Okay," Maggie murmurs.

The session has gone way overtime, and Dr. Fuentes leads us back to the waiting room. She shakes hands with both of us and says to Maggie, "Beautiful people attract beautiful friends."

That, Nbook, is her good-bye.

Homeroom

Yesterday, as we leave the session with Dr. Fuentes, everything seems fine. Maggie's <u>happy</u>. Her smile is back. I realize I'd practically forgotten what it looked like.

Ducky's waiting for us outside and she flies into the car.

"So, how'd it go?" he asks.

"Fine," Maggie says. "She's a good therapist, Ducky. For future reference."

She doesn't go into detail. And Ducky doesn't pry. I give him credit for that.

Well, we're all in a good mood until we reach Maggie's neighborhood. Somewhere around Pine Canyon Road, her smile disappears.

Ducky and I both notice it. We start telling jokes. Trying to lighten it up.

But when she gets out of the car and says good-bye, her face is all glum. She's worried.

She's home.

I can tell she'd rather be anywhere else in the world.

Later on, I call Dawn and tell her what happened. Dawn is amazed that

I stayed for the session, but she's glad I did. She tells me I'm a great friend.

I don't see Maggie again until this morning at the lockers. She's subdued. She mentions that she likes Dr. Fuentes but doesn't seem to want to say much more than that.

I hope this works, Nbook.

I hope the atmosphere at her house doesn't ruin everything.


Study hall

Brendan spots me with you in homeroom, Nbook.

The bell has already rung and I'm still writing.

He's not snooping or anything, just waiting for me.

When I finish he asks, "Are you okay? You're looking sad."

"I'm fine."

"And you didn't say hi. You always say hi." He smiles. "Even to me."

"Just . . . busy," I say. "With plans for the Homecoming Bash."

Which isn't totally true. (Yet. But it <u>will</u> be.)

We walk out of class together. He's being so friendly to me. And when we start talking about Vanish, he's totally enthusiastic. Asking all about our set list and saying nice things about the tape. I can tell he's trying to cheer me up.

Unless it's more than that.

Do you think he's flirting with me, Nbook?

Should I care?

Nahh.

He's a guy. He fits the qualifications for my No-Guys policy. Nothing he says will make a difference. One James is enough for a lifetime.

That's not fair. Brendan does seem a lot nicer than James.

Although <u>James</u> seemed a lot nicer than James at first.

So you never know.

Oh. Later on, Cece asks me why I'm so hostile to Brendan.

(Can you believe this, Nbook? She was spying on us.)

I tell her I wasn't hostile. I didn't _feel_ hostile. Maybe matter-of-fact, that's all.

She says Brendan's cute. And nice. And she's _positive_ he likes me.

I tell her I'm not in a boyfriend mode.

Hey, if _she's_ interested, I won't stand in the way.

But she's not.

At least I don't think so.

Rehearsal

Oh, Nbook. I don't know what's going on.

I don't believe in miracle cures. I'm a realistic person.

But shouldn't Maggie be feeling a _little_ better?

I mean, we have not gotten

through _one_ whole song without stopping for her.

Her throat's dry.

The keyboard keys are sticky.

She's forgotten the words. The cues.

She can't hit the high notes.

The Homecoming Bash is in 10 days. We're supposed to be getting _tighter_.

Maybe the garage is too crowded and noisy. Dawn's here. Marina. Bruce's cousins from Fresno. Patti's parents.

Should I throw everyone out?

No. This is a _rock band_ — they're _supposed_ to perform for noisy crowds.

Maybe it's Justin. Is _he_ making her nervous?

WHAT'S GOING ON?

Dawn is shooting me looks.

I'm going to talk to her. Don't go away.


Sorry. Didn't mean to be gone so long.

LOTS to report.

First. I meet Dawn at the trough,

where the Chavezes are setting up for break. And eating. The band is in the middle of "Fallen Angel."

Dawn's about to say something, but the music suddenly stops.

"Sorry! Sorry!" Maggie calls out. She's massaging her neck, looking pained. "My fault."

Rico's removing his guitar strap. He seems tired. "Let's break, guys, okay?"

Everyone heads to the trough.

Except Maggie. She's at the keyboard. Just sitting.

Dawn and I walk over to her.

i know, i know, i sound terrible. you don't have to tell me.

Dawn tries to talk to her. I try to talk to her.

Nothing works. She's a nervous wreck about the Bash. Which she is now calling her "professional debut."

She's magnifying this, Nbook. She's digging herself into such a deep hole, I don't know how she'll get out.

Now Justin decides to get into the act. He's walking toward us now, a half-eaten doughnut in his hand.

I figure, (former crush) + (junk food) = (just what Maggie doesn't need).

But he's being very sweet. Saying don't worry, you sound great, you look great, you're going to steal the show, yada yada.

Dawn and I jump on the pro-Maggie bandwagon. We're all complimenting her. Persisting. Maggie's nodding her head, listening hard.

At one point Justin gently touches

her arm. "Hey, just let the music take control."

She flinches a little. (What's <u>with</u> these two, Nbook?)

Soon the band heads back. Rico plays the opening chords to "Hey, Down There."

And Maggie misses her entrance.

Dawn and I are looking at each other. The Homecoming Bash is crashing before my eyes.

Then the song starts again.

Maggie's stiff as a plank. She looks as if she's taking a math exam. But something happens when she begins the lyric.

Maybe it's because she wrote it. Maybe it's the topic — a girl who can't give herself comfort and love until she steps outside herself.

Whatever. As the emotion takes over, Maggie leans into the keyboard. Her eyes close but her fingers aren't missing a note.

The chatting in the garage peters out. Then it stops.

Maggie's voice is soaring. The words are ringing clear and urgent, yet somehow they sound like a whisper in deepest confidence.

I'm so swept up, I don't want the song to end.

And when it does, the garage is dead silent.

Maggie's hands are resting on the last chord, her eyes still closed.

When she opens them, she looks a little bewildered. As if she's just awoken from a dream in a place she didn't expect to be.

I think Justin is the first to start clapping.

I know I'm the first to cheer out loud.

But in a second, we're all screaming and whistling and stomping our feet.

Rico plants a big wet one on Maggie's cheek. She's turning red.

"She did it!" Dawn yells.

I have to sit down. The tension has turned me into a sack of jangled nerves.

But I'm relieved.

For the first time all night, I'm thinking, <u>she can do it.</u>

You know what? The rest of the songs are just as good. The band even plays through the scheduled break (and they <u>never</u> miss a trip to the trough).

When I call the end of rehearsal, we give them a standing ovation.

"You finally got your mojo working!" Mr. Chavez shouts.

Must be some '70s term. (NOTE TO ME: Find out what a mojo is.)

Everyone's happy. Maggie's happy.

I'm <u>really</u> happy. Mainly because of Maggie. But also because of the band.

I <u>HATE</u> to admit this, Nbook. But I haven't heard them sound this good since James was kicked out. For the first time, I don't miss his playing.

So I'm dancing around, praising everybody, telling them the Homecoming Bash is going to be fantastic.

And for some reason, I start thinking about Brendan.

I don't know why.

Then I see Maggie. She's talking to Justin and Dawn.

She's beaming.

Thank God.

Hey. Remember me, Nbook?

Don't be hurt. After last week, I needed a break from writing.

OK. Update. The latest headlines:

FLASH!

VANISH LOOKING GOOD

Friday's rehearsal sizzles. Saturday is a little ragged. Sunday we rest, Monday we're hot again.

Only 3 more days, Nbook!

Maggie's singing much better. Still slipping in and out, though. Saturday's

rough for her. Some big fight between
Mr. and Mrs. Blume the night before,
I gather.

Anyway, right after "This Is War,"
I discover

### FLASH!
### JUSTIN STILL CARES
About Maggie, that is. He leans
over to me as Rico's tuning his guitar
and asks, "Is she okay?"

He's got this really concerned look
in his eyes.

Last week I suspected he liked
her. Now I'm sure.

Hmmm. Maybe Maggie will get a
second chance with him after
all.

Anyway, I tell Justin that Maggie's
fine.

And in case you're wondering . . .

# FLASH!
## FUENTES STILL MAJOR FORCE IN BLUME'S LIFE

Well, a force, anyway.

Before Friday's session, though, Maggie almost freaks out. Papi has said I can't go with her because Tio Luis is taking the family out to Café Con Leche. Mami says that Maggie should go by herself anyway.

Breaking the news to Maggie is not easy. But she ends up going. And surviving just fine.

And going back on Monday.

She says she's not feeling much of an improvement yet, but she's learning a lot about herself. Dr. Fuentes is helping her plan meals with the advice of a nutritionist.

(Oh. Guess what? I finally ask how she's paying for this. Turns out her father is paying. Maggie just tells him she's seeing a therapist and he doesn't bat an eye. She does not, however, tell him <u>why</u> she's going.)

I wish she were eating more by now. She's not.

Which is frustrating.

You know, Nbook, sometimes I still don't get it. I mean, eating seems so easy. Like walking. Or breathing.

Maggie can play the piano. Ace math exams. Sing.

But a simple thing like put-food-in-mouth?

I guess it's just not so simple for some people. Maybe I'll never fully understand it.

I just tell myself: If she needs to take it slow, she needs to take it slow.

At least she's on the right track.

Oh. One last

### Flash

(Just a mini.)

BRENDAN IS NO LONGER A GUY

Guys are in the doghouse.

Brendan has moved out.

In my estimation, he has risen to another level.

He has become a Pal. Pals have

certain qualities not found in mere Guys.

They don't deceive. They don't think only about themselves. They listen. They're thoughtful and friendly and have senses of humor.

They're more like girls.

Not that Brendan is like a girl. He's not. It's just that in the quality of his personality — <u>why am I explaining this to myself? I know what I mean!</u>

Anyway, the other day, Brendan brings me a tape. A mix he's made.

"What's this for?" I ask.

"Just paying you back for the Vanish tape," he says.

Nice, huh?

<u>That's</u> what I mean.

He's different in homeroom too. Not so stiff and shy. Lately he slips me these corny notes. Jokes like, "When it comes to homeroom, I can take it or Leavitt."

Real groaners, but that's okay. They're cute.

Plus, he likes my friends. Especially

Sunny, who flirts with him (when she's actually _in_ homeroom, which isn't that often). When I introduce him to Maggie, he's thrilled. He loved her voice on the tape. (And, believe it or not, he has never _heard_ of Hayden Blume, which makes Maggie appreciate him even more.)

I don't want to make a big deal of this, Nbook. I just mean to say that he's a change of pace from the guys that have become familiar to me at Vista.

It's refreshing to be around someone who's newer in the school than I am. It's good for my self-esteem.

Thurs., 10/8
4:35 P.M.

Nbook, I am RED.
FURIOUS.
Look at this. Look what I find today
in my locker:

YUKON RUN BUT YUKON TIED!
—U NO WHO

Like I need this?

Two days before our biggest concert. Two days before my debut as manager of a _professional_ rock group. When I have to worry about buying spare electrical cords. Fixing mikes. Making sure the risers are set up. Keeping my best friend (and lead singer) happy and healthy.

AAAAAAGGGH!

This is not cute, James Kodaly.

Why do I bother keeping his notes, Nbook? Am I perverse or what?

I know why I do it. Because I might need them. As evidence. For something. I don't know what.

Oh. You know what the translation is? "You can run but you can't hide." It takes me practically the whole day to figure that out.

Oh so sweet. He sure knows how to win a girl's heart.

Whenever I see James in the hall, I feel angry. I can't even look at him.

He acts as if nothing has happened.

Jerk.

Creep.
Sicko.
Okay. Enough space wasted. This topic is closed.

From here on out, all I will think about is the Homecoming Bash.

Fri. 10/9
Soc. Stud.

The mike's not ready at the shop. No spares.

Risers are too small. Will have to move some of the equipment onto the dance floor.

Rico's home with a cold.

Oh. And we're going to have to set up around cheerleading practice! (Can you believe this?!)

'Bye. Gotta pretend to study.

Before lunch I call Rico. He'll be OK. Also, his dad has an old mike left over from <u>his</u> band. But I'm still worried as I walk to lunch.

Dawn and Maggie are waiting for me, and we get in line. I must be complaining pretty loudly, because behind us I hear, "What happened? Aren't you guys going to play?"

It's Brendan. He's sliding his tray down the line, next to mine.

"I mean, I don't want to go to the Bash if you're not playing," he explains.

I tell him everything'll work out. Then I start loading my tray.

I glance ahead at Maggie. She has taken a folded sheet of paper from her pocket. She reads it carefully, then chooses a cup of soup, a green salad, and a bread stick.

Progress.

As we leave the line, Brendan and Maggie are chatting about music. Maggie asks him to sit with us.

He looks totally flustered. Like, <u>who, little old me</u>?

I say, "What's the matter? Haven't you ever eaten lunch with a star?"

Maggie elbows me.

I run to grab a table.

Brendan sits next to me. Mostly we talk about the Bash.

I'm in a crazy mood. Feisty.

Dawn says she's glad it isn't a <u>date</u> kind of party.

"Ends up being the same, only the guys don't have to buy flowers," I say. "That's the only thing I'll miss. Flowers."

Maggie says it would be perfect if the guys brought the flowers anyway, but it was still a non-date party.

I say why not just have them bring the flowers, then go home.

Soon we're laughing a lot. But Brendan's looking lost and uncomfortable, so Maggie starts asking him questions. Where did you live, etc. I, the big mouth, end up answering some of them.

Brendan lets me. He doesn't say much at all. He never likes to talk about himself or his family. Just music.

The boy still needs to loosen up, Nbook.

We'll work on him.


Language Arts

The Maggie Morph continues.

Before class you could mistake her for Cece: "So, did you see how Brendan was looking at you in lunch? How disappointed he was when we were dissing date parties? How he laughed at all your jokes? How he couldn't keep his eyes off you," etc. etc.

Part of me is thinking, Dr. Fuentes is a genius.

But part of me prefers the <u>quiet</u> Maggie.

Frankly, with everything that's on my mind, I'm in no mood for hints and gossip.

"Do you think I care about stuff like that?" I say. "I have enough to worry about."

Maggie acts as if I've slapped her.

I understand. I'm—I'm really sorry, Amalia.

Sorry for what?

For being part of "enough to worry about."

I didn't mean it that way!

But it's true, Amalia. You've been the best friend. But you have to think of yourself now. You can't give up your own life to help your friends with their problems.

Maggie says this, Nbook.
Maggie.
And you know what?
She's right.

It's here.
We're in the gym.

Home
6:19 P.M.

OK. Deep breaths.
   Approx. 11 minutes before I have to
go back to school.
   The equipment fits (yea!). It's a
little cramped, but we'll live.

Everybody's home changing. I'm wearing my black scoopback spandex dress. Won't show dust & dirt. Show starts at 8. Have to be there by 7 at the latest. Guess where Mr. and Mrs. Chavez take us out to dinner after setup? Mexican Kitchen. (WRONG kind of food for a nervous stomach.) They invite Ducky and Dawn, because they've helped us and have been big fans.

Ducky can't go. Doesn't say why.

Justin sits at a table near restaurant door. He's smiling at Maggie, but she doesn't see him & sits at next table.

I think, Is she ignoring him on purpose? Who knows?

I sit w/ her and notice veget. section of menu. "Lite meals for lite appetites."

But Maggie just orders green salad and bottled water.

And when it comes, she barely eats any.

And I'm thinking, Oh no.

Everyone's talking at once. Making toasts. Laughing. Bruce is wild. Singing. Shouting, "We're kings of the world!" Patti announces that the Homecoming Bash is due to "one person only, Amalia Vargas" and everyone stands and cheers.

But I'm still concerned about Maggie. She's getting worse.

WHY WON'T SHE EAT? She needs to. I can't have her passing out onstage.

I want to say something, but I don't want to upset her. Not today.

She gives me a look. "Are you OK?"

"Fine."

She leans over and whispers, "Amalia, I know what you're thinking. Relax. This time it is nerves, OK? I just don't want my dinner to end up on the risers!"

She's smiling.

I believe her.

I have to stop worrying.

OK.

Time 2 go.

NBOOK, THIS IS IT.

I'm numb, Nbook.

Exhausted.

But I can't sleep.

I'm afraid of sleep. I may wake up tomorrow to find it was a dream, and I'll have to do it all over again.

And if I do, it won't turn out the same.

It couldn't possibly.

So it's you and me, Nbook. Until dawn if necessary.

Then, if it is a dream, I'll have it on paper. So I can read it again and again and know how it felt.

It starts out horrible.

We get to the gym and I'm a wreck.

Christina McDonnell tells us that the cheerleaders have moved their practice to the auditorium. That's the good news.

Things go downhill from there.

I'm ready to call it quits and head home.

Meanwhile kids are starting to arrive. Are they supposed to be here? No. Are my door people telling them they should wait till 8:00? No.

Christina is stepping in now. Both of us are running around, solving problems, signing papers, giving orders, bossing kids around.

"Out! Out!" I'm shouting, herding kids away like cattle.

No one's listening.

My fuse is burning short. I'm about to say things I wouldn't write on your clean pages, Nbook.

And then the crowd opens up, and he's standing there.

Smiling.

It's a direct smile. Open. Not off to the side. Not shy.

And it changes him.

Then I notice the outfit. A gorgeous dark-patterned shirt and baggy black pants.

Hardly any of the other guys have

dressed up for this party.

Brendan has. And he looks totally cool.

But my eyes fix on a flower he's holding. A long-stemmed rose.

Now, roses are boring. But I've never seen a color like this. A kind of peach, with hints of red and pink and amber.

It's stunning.

I know I'm supposed to shoo him out. But I can't.

"Nice," I say.

Then I see the rose coming closer. And I realize he's giving it to me.

He remembered what I said at lunch yesterday. About flowers.

I'm speechless.

People are now stampeding into the gym. Christina's running around doing all the work herself. Vanish is warming up fiercely. I know I have to be in a million other places.

But all I see is the rose and the smile, and they're both so beautiful, and I'm thinking, what does this mean? But I <u>know</u> what it means, it's obvious, and I realize everyone else has known it all along and why haven't I seen it in him before? And it's all so strange and confusing and exciting, I can't think of a word to say. So I just look at him.

Nbook, it's like I'm seeing someone new, someone I've never met, and I'm thinking:

Brendan?

<u>Brendan?</u>

What now? If I take the rose, does that make me his date? I think, Is this going to be like the ankle bracelet James gave me? Like, once I wear it, I become his property?

No. Brendan is not James. Brendan is sweet.

But <u>James</u> was sweet when I first met him too.

"AMALIA!"

Rico's voice shocks me into reality. I have a concert to run.

"I have to go," I say.

I turn and race toward the band. I feel the blood rushing to my face.

"WHERE's MAGGIE?" Bruce is shouting.

<u>Maggie</u>.

Maggie should be at the keyboard, but her seat is empty.

Patti is near the door, pointing into the hallway.

I'm out there in a second. Room 134 is open. Our dressing room.

Maggie's inside. Staring into the mirror. She's plastered her face with a pale shade of pancake.

When I'm closer, I realize she doesn't have any makeup on. That's the color of her skin.

"What's up?" I'm trying to sound loose and calm, but my voice is tight and edgy.

I CAN'T MY VOICE IS GONE MY HAIR'S DRY I LOOK DISGUSTING THERE ARE TOO MANY PEOPLE PLEASE JUST DO INSTRUMENTALS...

No.

This is not happening.

Maggie is a wreck.

I try to give her a shoulder rub. I tell her she's going to be great.

But she's stiff and silent. Which makes *me* panic.

That's all she needs. A frantic manager pummeling her shoulders.

Easy, Vargas, I say to myself. You're supposed to be the calm one.

I let go of her poor back. I count to 10. And then I sit down next to her.

She's staring at me. She looks like

she's about to cry. "Amalia, I can't do this."

I'm searching my brain for the right thing to say. Trying to remember pearls of wisdom from Dr. Fuentes. <u>Anything</u> that might work.

And then I remember one thing that did. Something that Justin had said.

I tell her to let the music take control.

She turns away. She's in some other world. I don't know if she's even heard me.

Outside, the band's warm-up has stopped.

We hear Christina's voice over the gym loudspeaker. She's quieting the crowd.

Rico peeks into the room and asks if everything's OK.

"Girls only!" I snap.

Now Christina is thanking the committees, the teachers, the administration . . .

"We're starting," I say to Maggie.

She stands and walks toward the

door. She looks so fragile, I almost want to pull her back. But the rest of the band is waiting outside, and they're applauding her and chanting, "Mag-gie! Mag-gie! Mag-gie!"

I'm right behind her as we walk into the gymnasium.

From where we're standing, in the doorway, we can see Christina's back and not much else. The crowd is hidden by the risers and the equipment.

"And now, what you've all been waiting for," Christina announces. "Vista's very own . . . Vanish!"

"YEAAAHHHH!" Bruce shouts, leaping onto the platform.

Patti follows him, raising her drumsticks high.

Rico's next.

The crowd is hollering.

Soon Patti's beating out the tempo for "This Is War." Bruce attacks the bass line.

"Knock 'em dead," I say to Maggie.

But she's frozen in place. She won't move.

It's as if this week never happened. The sensational rehearsals, the incredible singing — down the toilet. She's forgotten them.

"Go!" I practically push her through the door.

Rico pulls Maggie up onto the platform. I hear a swell of cheering.

My heart is beating so hard I think it's going to come loose.

Maggie sits at the keyboard.

She misses her entrance.

Now I'm dying.

Rico is smiling patiently. Bruce is in his own world. They're vamping now. Waiting for her.

Then Maggie's fingers strike the keyboard. The opening chord.

And she starts singing.

She sounds tense. Unsure.

But she's doing it. She's there.

I sneak around the side of the platform. Now I can see the crowd. A group has gathered in front of the band. The Vanish groupies.

Some kids are dancing in small

clumps, but most everyone's at the food table.

Maggie's starting to look sick.

I move in closer. I elbow my way past the groupies.

Then her eyes slowly close.

She's passing out.

Panic.

I begin to vault onto the risers. But I stop myself.

I realize she's not sick. She's just feeling the music. She's singing with strength. Passion.

I take deep breaths. I try to enjoy this.

The next song is even better.

By "Hey, Down There," Maggie is her old self again.

She's <u>rocking</u> by the time they do "Friday Night Blues."

Me? I'm screaming. Dancing with myself.

Then Rico calls "Fallen Angel."

<u>Dumb choice</u>, I'm thinking.

The crowd is worked up.

You're supposed to give them

another up-tempo tune, not a soft
ballad. I've trained them to do this.
(But who am I, Nbook? Just the
manager.)

The song begins and I can feel
the energy in the gym start to dip.

Kids are drifting away, talking and
laughing.

In the corner of the gym, Christina
is dimming the lights. Trying to create
a mood.

<u>Good luck</u>, I think.

Then I hear Maggie's voice.


<u>Down to earth,</u>
<u>Feet on the ground,</u>
<u>I look straight ahead,</u>
<u>Don't turn around.</u>
<u>In all I do,</u>
<u>I'm here for you;</u>
<u>I'm your fallen angel</u> . . .


Nbook, my jaw is dropping open.

Maggie doesn't sound good. She
sounds <u>phenomenal</u>. Her voice is soft
but intense. It's as if she's making the

song up on the spot. Out of her own
emotions. Surrounding the words with
her soul.

I'm so caught up, I almost don't
notice what's happening around me.

The chattering and laughing have
dwindled away.

At the food tables, people are
turning to face the band.

To face Maggie.

Now some couples are pairing off.
They're slow dancing.

I suddenly realize I've been
clutching Brendan's rose this whole
time.

I look around for him, but he's
nowhere.

Which makes sense. I figure he's
gone home. Or maybe he's found
another girl. Someone who didn't run
away from him.

I realize I shouldn't have taken
the rose. He could have given it to
her.

Oh, well.

Soon the band is playing "Hey, Down

There" with the new, reggae beat. Then "Slow Down."

When Maggie sings "Dust off your heart/Take it off the shelf/And don't forget to love yourself," I'm all choked up. She's singing about herself, Nbook. And if I'm not mistaken, she's believing it.

For the last two numbers, Rico calls for the rockers "No Retreat" and "Just in Time."

The mood change is amazing.

Everyone's going wild.

When the set is over, the place explodes.

Cheers. Screaming. Stomping on the floor.

I'm ecstatic. Laughing and crying at the same time.

Someone behind me starts calling out Maggie's name. It spreads through the whole gym, until the rhythm of the stomps matches the rhythm of the chant.

Maggie looks flabbergasted. Dazed. She's still sitting at the keyboard.

Justin is calling out to her, "Take a bow!"

She hears him and stands up. Then she does this prim little curtsy that Mrs. Knudsen must have taught her to use after piano recitals.

It's totally wrong. But the crowd doesn't care.

They're roaring for her.

Maggie is beaming now. Soaking it up. Waving.

When she steps off the platform, I throw my arms around her. Nbook, I am so PROUD.

"Was I OK?" is the first thing she asks.

I burst out laughing, "Can't you tell?"

She smiles. "I guess."

"LET'S GIVE IT UP FOR VANISH!" shouts the DJ, who's already spinning tunes.

Bruce, Patti, and Rico are leaping off the platform now. It's pure pandemonium.

Then, from behind me, I hear Christina calling out, "Congratulations!"

I turn. I'm about to thank her, but I notice she's looking at my right hand.

"What's that?" she asks.

The rose.

It's bent now, but still beautiful.

I tell her somebody gave it to me.

"Lucky," she says with this big, knowing smile. "I wish someone would give _me_ a rose like that."

For a moment I feel about nine feet tall.

I mean, not long ago I'm feeling like the lowest form of life in Vista. And now the most popular girl in school is jealous of _me_.

As she moves on to congratulate Maggie, I realize something.

I have to see Brendan.

To thank him. To apologize and explain.

Because Christina is right.

I am lucky.

Very lucky.

I run over to the food table, but he's not there.

I circle around the gym. No Brendan.

I look into every group of kids. My stomach is sinking and I'm realizing I have blown it and I'm a complete fool, when I spot a couple dancing in the corner.

I've been introduced to the girl. I think her name's Cheryl.

The guy she's with is James.

After all this time, all the notes and weird behavior, he's finally found somebody else.

I'm relieved.

I'm also horrified. Cheryl doesn't deserve the treatment I got.

I want to run to her. Warn her

away. But I know how James would react to that.

I figure I'll catch her alone sometime.

James swings around. He's facing my direction.

I duck away so he won't see me. A nearby exit door is open, so I slip outside.

I'm about to walk past a guy sitting on the bottom step, but I stop short.

It's Brendan.

My breath catches.

He doesn't notice me. He's looking off toward the pond, lost in his own world. His face is glum.

He's mad at me.

I hold the rose behind my back. "Hey," I call out.

He turns. He springs to his feet.

"Nice night," he says.

He's smiling. He doesn't look angry at all.

I'm so grateful and relieved, I don't know what to say. So I just start babbling.

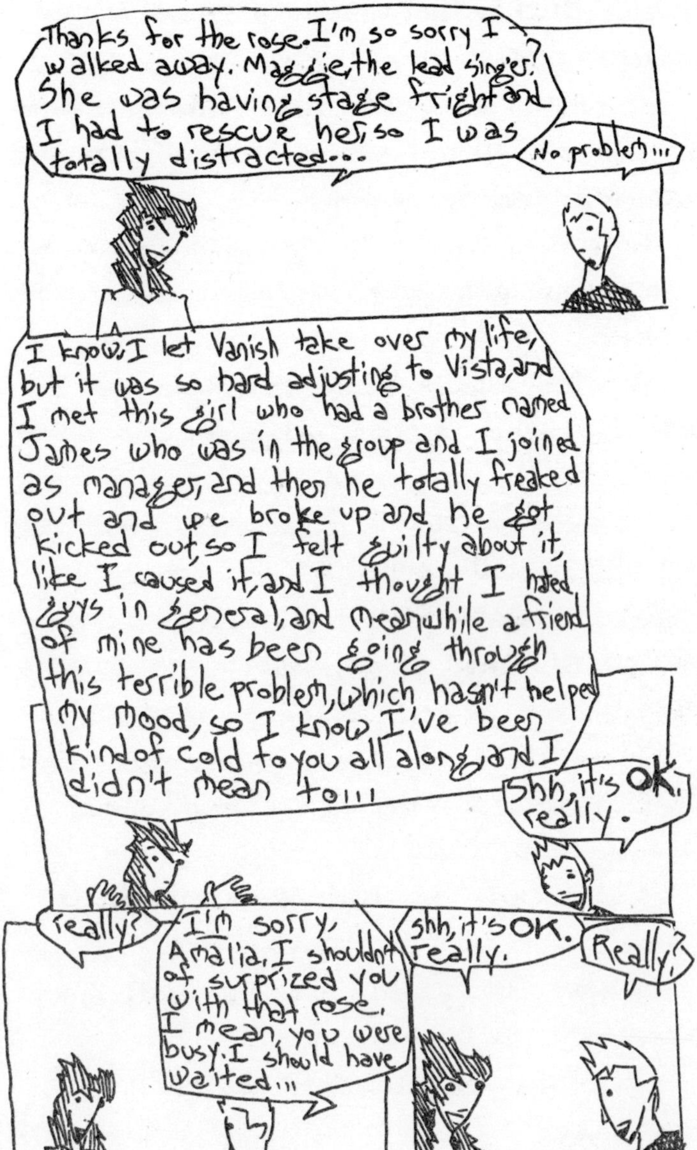
Thanks for the rose. I'm so sorry I walked away. Maggie, the lead singer? She was having stage fright and I had to rescue her, so I was totally distracted...
No problem...
I know, I let Vanish take over my life, but it was so hard adjusting to Vista, and I met this girl who had a brother named James who was in the group and I joined as manager, and then he totally freaked out and we broke up and he got kicked out, so I felt guilty about it, like I caused it, and I thought I hated guys in general, and meanwhile a friend of mine has been going through this terrible problem, which hasn't helped my mood, so I know I've been kind of cold to you all along, and I didn't mean to...
Shh, it's OK. really.
really?
I'm sorry, Amalia, I shouldn't of surprized you with that rose. I mean, you were busy. I should have waited...
shh, it's OK. really.
Really?

We both start laughing. And I realize <u>this</u> is one thing James and I never did. Laugh at each other. Laugh <u>with</u> each other. Laugh, period. Maybe that was our problem.

Was.

James is <u>was</u> now.

Brendan is <u>is</u>.

In the green-blue of his eyes I see sky and water. No limits. No places to hide.

I see myself in there too. <u>Me</u>. Not an idea of a girlfriend. Not some trophy to make him look good.

It's thrilling, Nbook.

Still, I'm frightened.

I mean, the sky is dangerous. So's the water. I don't know what I'm heading into.

All I know is that I trust him, Nbook.

Maybe it's stupid, but I feel I've known him my whole life.

And that makes him worth a try. Doesn't it?

Anyway, all this is running through

my head, and I hardly notice a slow love song has begun.

Brendan has taken my hand. He asks if I want to dance.

I say yes. We walk back into the gym.

Brendan puts his arm around me. I don't really know how to slow dance. When he steps on my foot, I realize he doesn't either.

That's OK. We begin to rock gently to the beat, making sure to keep our feet to ourselves.

Nearby, James is dancing with Cheryl.

I spot Maggie. She's at the food table, talking to Justin.

Just beyond them, Rico and Christina are in a deep conversation.

Brendan suddenly asks if I'm feeling all right.

I realize I'm distracted. As usual, thinking about other people's happiness instead of my own.

I put my head on Brendan's shoulder. I can hear the soft beat of his heart. We're swaying now. I'm not sure if we're in rhythm to the music.

But it doesn't matter.

This is my happiness. This is my music.

Our music. No matter what our feet are doing, Brendan and I are in perfect sync.

I check on Maggie one more time. And Rico and Patti and Bruce. Just to make sure they're OK.

And then I close my eyes. And know I'm in good hands.

It's 2 A.M.
That's it, Nbook.
That's life.
To be continued.

# A Note to Readers

If you or someone you know might have an eating disorder, or if you want to know more about eating disorders and how to deal with them, the following organizations provide valuable help and information:

**American Anorexia/Bulimia Association**
165 W. 46th Street, Suite 1108
New York, NY 10036
(212) 575-6200
http://members.aol.com/AmAnBu
E-mail: AmAnBu@aol.com

**National Association of Anorexia Nervosa
and Associated Disorders**
P.O. Box 7
Highland Park, IL 60035
(847) 831-3438
E-mail: ANAD20@aol.com

**Anorexia Nervosa and Related Eating Disorders**
P.O. Box 5102
Eugene, OR 97405
(541) 344-1144
http://www.anred.com

**Eating Disorders Awareness and Prevention**
603 Stewart Street, Suite 803
Seattle, WA 98101
(206) 382-3587
http://members.aol.com/edapinc

# About the Author

ANN MATTHEWS MARTIN was born on August 12, 1955. She grew up in Princeton, NJ, with her parents and her younger sister, Jane.

Although Ann used to be a teacher and then an editor of children's books, she's now a full-time writer. She gets the ideas for her books from many different places. Some are based on personal experiences. Others are based on childhood memories and feelings. Many are written about contemporary problems or events.

All of Ann's characters are made up. But some of her characters are based on real people. Sometimes Ann names her characters after people she knows; other times she chooses names she likes.

In addition to California Diaries, Ann Martin has written many other books, including the Baby-sitters Club series. She has written twelve novels for young people, including *Missing Since Monday, With You or Without You, Slam Book,* and *Just a Summer Romance.*

Ann M. Martin does not live in California, though she does visit frequently. She lives in New York with her cats, Gussie, Woody, and Willy. Her hobbies are reading, sewing, and needlework — especially making clothes for children.

# Ducky, Diary Two

"Is something going on? Something you want to talk about?"

The words sound so weak, so wimpy. But you're trying, you're NOT GIVING UP.

Alex keeps his eyes straight ahead. He looks as if he's thinking about what to say, shaping an answer.

But he just yawns. "You wouldn't understand."

Slap.

What now, Ducky?

You're thinking: FINE, he wants to be that way? He wants to abuse his best friend? He can stay here alone.

See if the reeds understand. See if the birds understand.

You get up, ready to leave, but you catch yourself.

You look closely at his face.

He's not dissing you. He's telling you the truth. HIS truth.

He honestly believes you wouldn't understand.

And maybe he's right.